DISCARDED
Goshen Public Library

GOSHEN PUBLIC LIBRARY
601 SOUTH FIFTH STREET
GOSHEN, IN 46526-3994

Vespucci

Copyright © 1990 Editions La Joie de Lire, Geneva
Copyright © 1992 Creative Education, Inc.
123 South Broad Street, Mankato, MN 56001, USA
For the American Edition.

International Copyrights reserved in all countries.
Printed in Italy.

Library of Congress Cataloging-in-Publication Data

Klingel, Cynthia Fitterer.
 [Vespucci. English]
 Vespucci / author, Gerard Jaeger : adapted by Cindy Klingel :
translated by Patricia Hauduroy.
 Translation of: Vespucci.
   Summary: A biography of the fifteenth-century Italian scholar and
businessman who became a seafarer in middle age and first recognized
that the New World was indeed new.
   ISBN 0-88682-485-0
   1. Vespucci, Amerigo, 1451–1512—Juvenile literature.
   2. Explorers—America—Biography—Juvenile literature.
   3. Explorers—Spain—Biography—Juvenile literature.
   4. America—Discovery and exploration—Spanish—Juvenile literature.
 [1. Vespucci, Amerigo, 1451–1512. 2. Explorers.] I. Jaeger, Gerard A.
Vespucci.   II. Title.
E125.V5K45   1991
970.01′6′092—dc20   [B]   91-19936

VESPUCCI

ILLUSTRATIONS BY
JOHN HOWE

STORY BY
GERARD JAEGER

TRANSLATED BY PATRICIA HAUDUROY
ADAPTED BY CINDY KLINGEL

CREATIVE EDUCATION

JB
Vespucci

While the ships of Christopher Columbus sailed down the Rio Tinto to the sea, a man lingered on the Palos quay. He gazed intently at the western horizon where no man had ever ventured. His name was Amerigo Vespucci, and nothing on that morning of August 3, 1492, foretold that his name would become a part of American history.

Amerigo Vespucci was born in Florence, Italy, on March 9, 1451. His parents, wishing him to follow a commercial career, sent him to St. Mark's Convent where he studied until he was twenty-six years old. Amerigo then left Italy and went to Paris, where he lived for about twelve years.

Although Amerigo was successful in Paris, he longed to sail the oceans in the wake of Christopher Columbus. Columbus was searching for a way to reach India, the land of spices, that would avoid the Constantinople route, which had been controlled by the Turks since 1453. Furthermore, having promised to find new possessions for the Spanish king, Columbus wanted to discover the islands spoken of by seagoing people, and be the first person to follow the passage of the sun. Amerigo, too, had this desire to discover new lands.

STELLA POLARIS ARCTICVS

SPHÆRA SATVRNIVS

SPHÆRA VENERIVS

SPHÆRA MARTIS

SPHÆRA SOLARIS

Paris Roma Herusalem Eden Calicut

SPHÆRA LVNA

SPHÆRA MERCVRII

SPHÆRA IOVIS

STELLA POLARIS ANTARCTICVS

| ire XII | Alexandre V | Jean XXIII | Martin V | Eugene IV | Felix V |
| 1415 | 1409–1410 | 1410–1415 | 1417–1431 | 1431–1447 | 1439–1 |

> *I had come to Spain on business, but I quickly realized that my life's purpose could only be fulfilled overseas. Therefore, I made up my mind to set forth and discover the world.*

This thirst for the unknown consumed Vespucci. Ultimately, it led him to follow Columbus to the sea. On his first voyage, Amerigo embarked with former companions of Columbus. When Amerigo reached the islands that Columbus had recently discovered, he learned of the pillaging of riches and the massacre of the native people. Because he deplored these acts, he made up his mind to sail his ships in exploration but not in conquest of the new lands.

As he sailed, Amerigo tried to understand these new lands, for they did not match any known description. During his nights on watch, he began to wonder if the cartographers had been mistaken in their description of the world. Columbus's calculations were based on the Greek cosmographer Ptolemy's image of the earth, which had been developed nine hundred years earlier. Amerigo began to doubt the maps and to follow his own intuition, his own beliefs about the lands and water bodies of the earth.

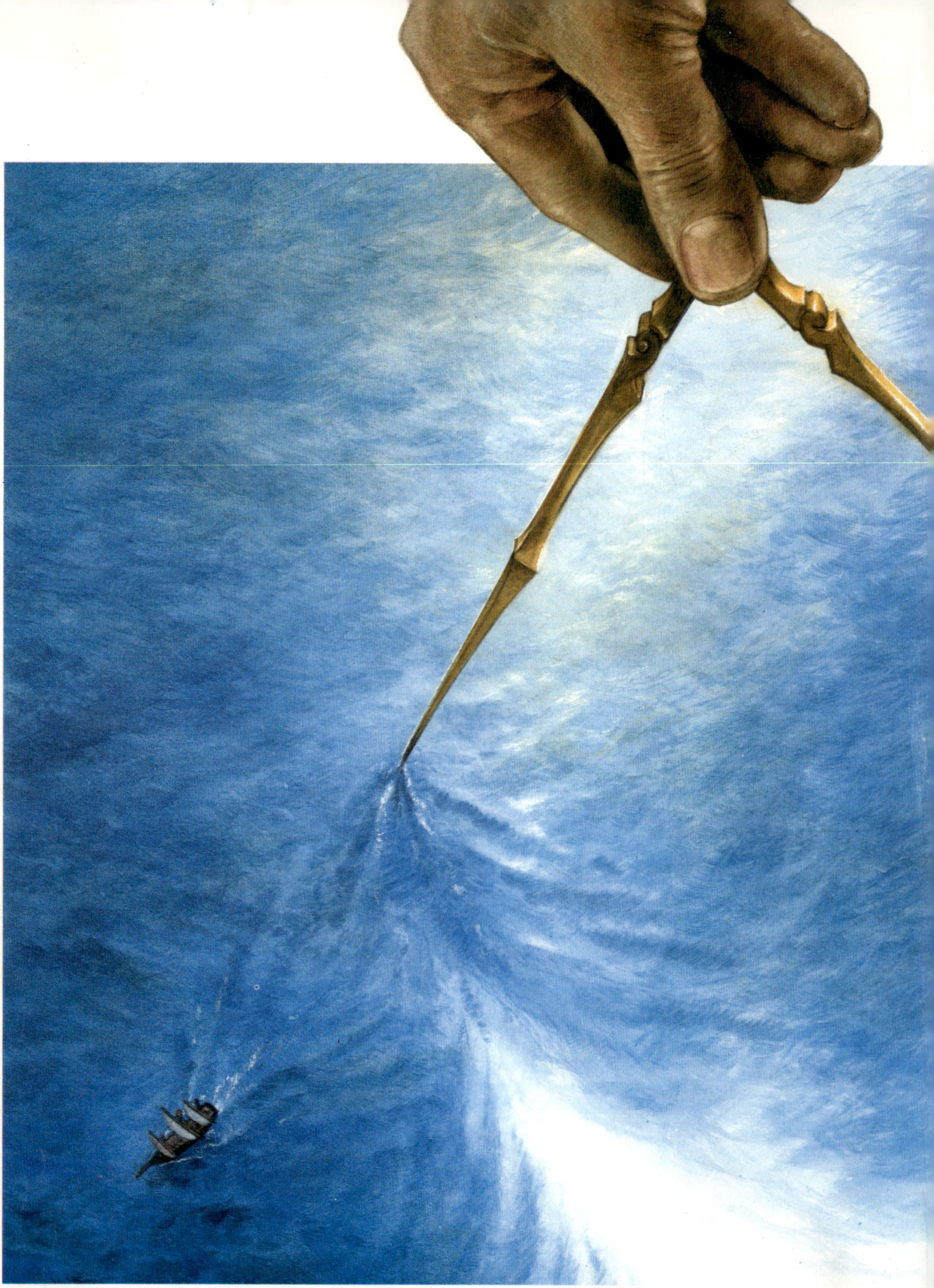

The more Amerigo navigated while observing the stars, the nearer he felt to the truth. His ideas, however, stood in sharp contrast to the men of his generation who still believed in the legends of imaginary lands. Some crew members hoped to catch sight of Atlantis, a place described in an ancient myth which had long filled the minds of Europeans with wonder. Others, influenced by Columbus, hoped to glimpse the legendary Antilla, which dated back to the maps of the Middle Ages. Sailing into the unknown made everything seem possible. However, the sailors began to fear that they would never see their homeland again, and the days went by filled with worries, and questions. Observing the wakes of their caravels—their ships—it was easy for the sailors to believe that the sea was closing in over them, to punish them for their foolhardiness.

The farther the ships sailed south, the nearer they came to land. Soon they reached the equator. Pushed by the prevailing winds, Amerigo and his crew had gone beyond the limits of the universe as imagined by the cartographers and poets. Amerigo's charts became useless, and most of the men expected to be thrown into the depths of Hell, as described in the Scriptures. Filled with anxiety over the unknown and exhilaration for the adventure, they pushed forward. This enthusiasm led them to not only complete this first voyage successfully, but undertake another. In a short three-year period, from 1497 to 1500, Vespucci and his shipmates completed two expeditions to sea for the king of Spain.

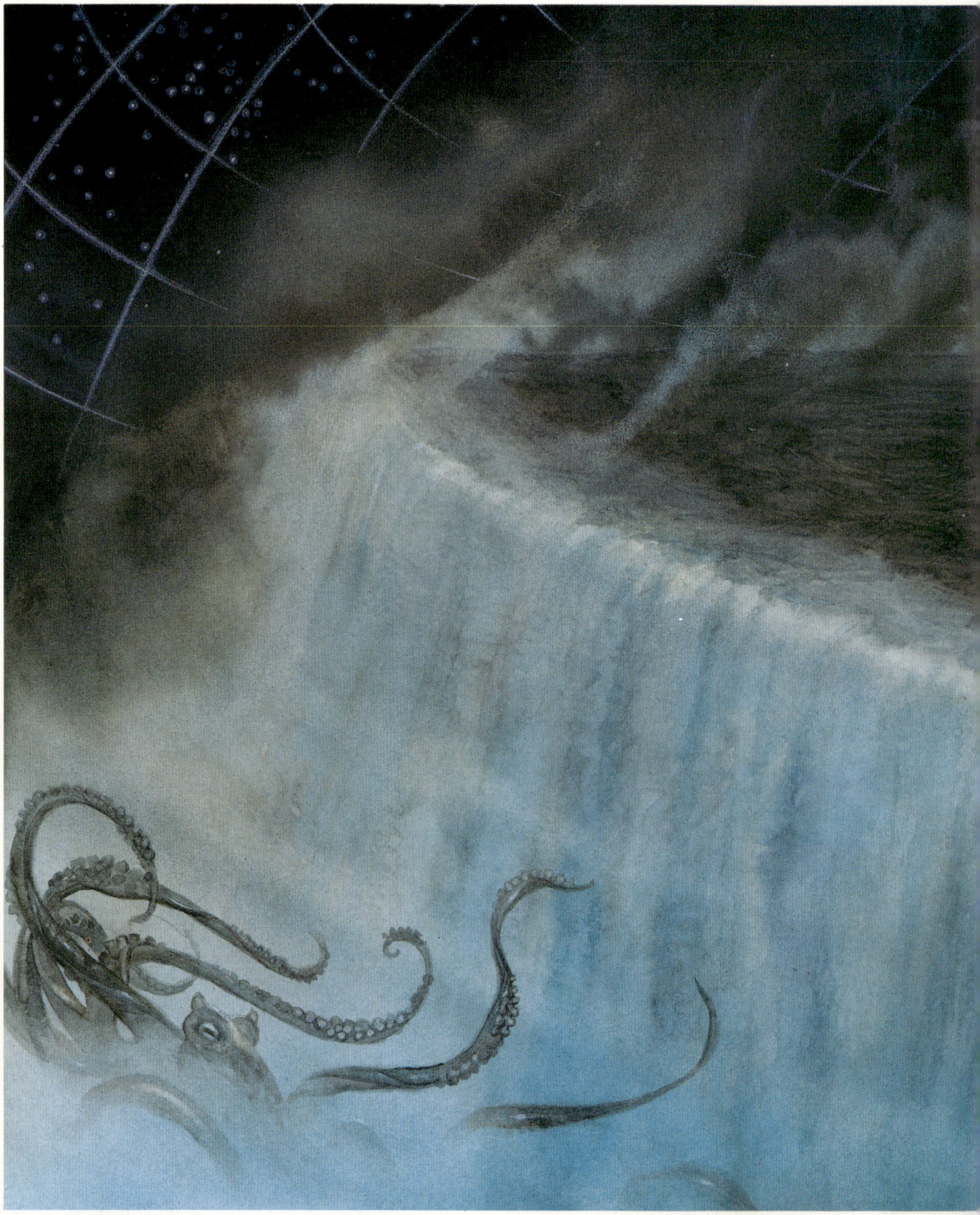

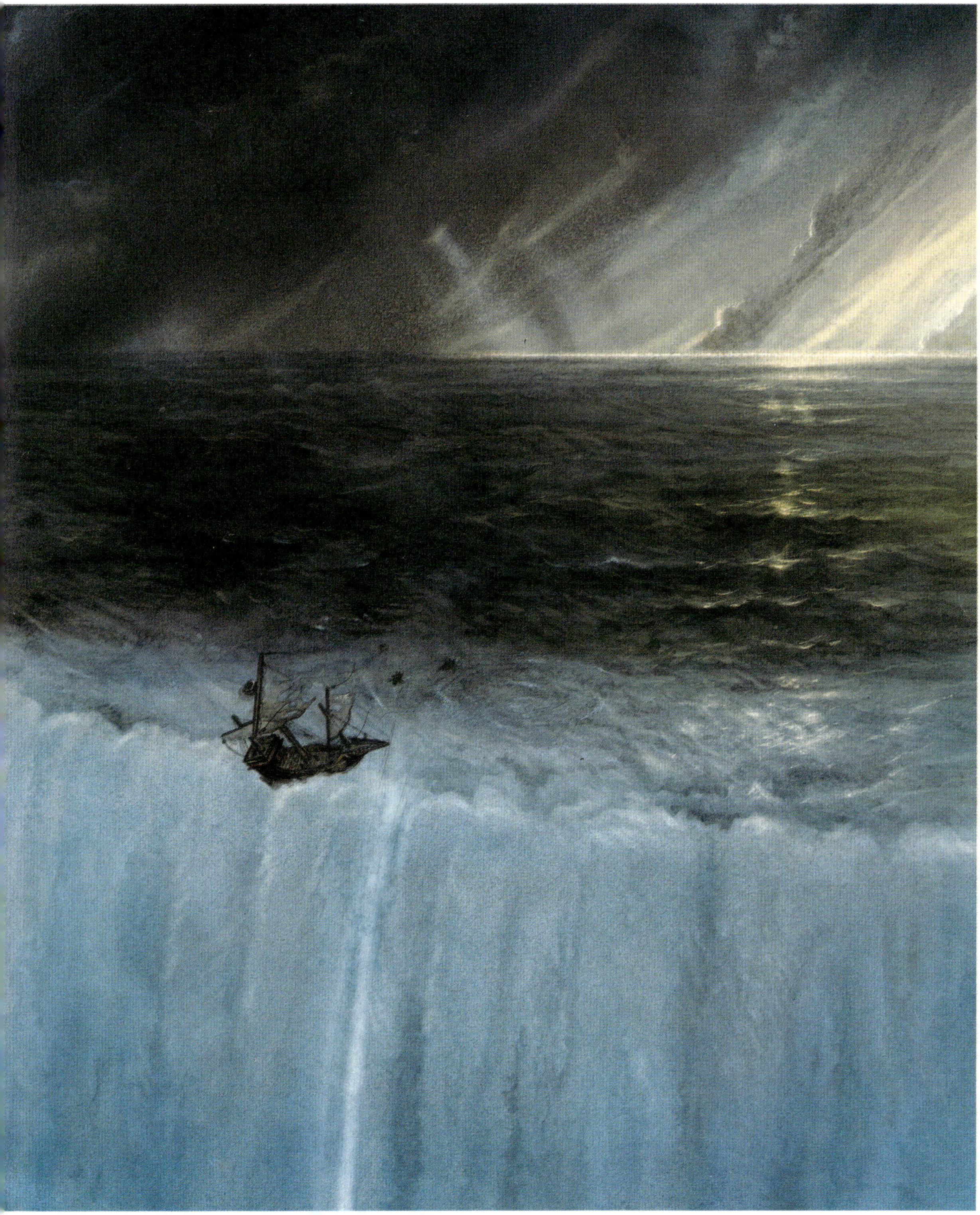

INFANTE·DOM~
HENRIQUE
1394~1460

talant de   bīe faire

On his return to Europe, Amerigo immediately started preparing for his third voyage. This time he intended to clear up the mystery of the piece of land which he suspected was a continent, and which he hadn't been able to explore properly on his earlier voyages. At the request of King Manuel of Portugal, Amerigo planned to sail the length of the coast of this new land until he reached a cape that he could go around, thereby proving that a land existed between Europe and the East Indies.

Only a few years prior to Amerigo's third voyage, Portuguese sailors had successfully explored the western coast of Africa. Convinced of the importance of maritime exploration, Henry the Navigator had gathered around him the most learned and well-read men of different cultures. In several years' time, by employing the best pilots and perfecting navigational skills and instruments, the Portuguese fleet had reached the Cape of Tempests and, in 1498, had succeeded in going around it. They had opened up a maritime route to the East Indies while the Spanish were establishing their first trading posts in the Caribbean. But the highly sought western route was yet to be discovered.

For Amerigo and his crew, the adventure began on May 10, 1501. On that day, they sailed forth on what would become the most dangerous voyage ever undertaken by man.

After leaving the maritime routes originally charted by the Spanish, Amerigo's sailors glimpsed a coast that they were the first to follow. At fifty degrees latitude south, the crew entered a world seeming to consist only of storms and winter; the nights became longer and longer until the sun disappeared completely. The continual downpours and whirlwinds made it impossible to go ashore.

On board, living conditions became more and more difficult. The food rotted, and water began running short. The men believed that dead men's souls haunted the ocean depths, because birds had stopped flying over the ships. The sails were in shreds, the yards had come apart in the strong winds, and the ship sent out long wrenching moans as it creaked, right up to the tops of the masts.

"The voyage lasted fifteen months and eleven days," wrote Vespucci. "During this time we sailed without seeing the ever-present Ursa Major or Minor. To plot our position and decide on our southern route, we couldn't use the stars of the other Pole which shone down on us in the shadows of the unknown."

At this time Amerigo was sailing in uncharted waters with nothing to guide him; all he had was his unshakable faith in his own destiny.

aquilo

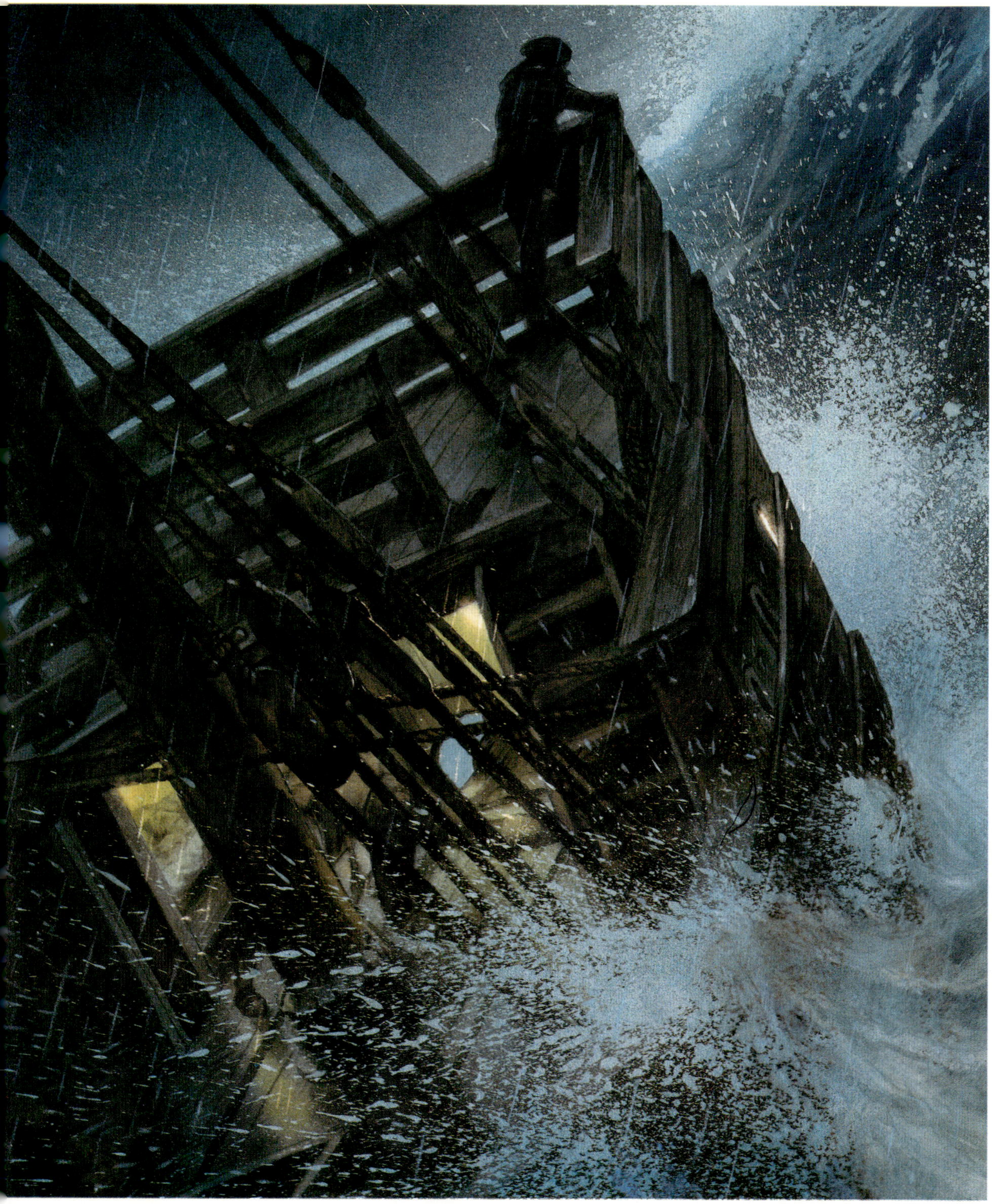

When the storms at last subsided, Amerigo ordered his captains to approach the coast in order to go ashore. They dropped anchor in a cove, and he sent several men to explore the land and investigate its inhabitants. Although Amerigo had strong beliefs, he was open-minded and accepting of other cultures. He valued people for what they were, regardless of the sometimes shocking differences between their ideas and standards and his own. This attitude of Amerigo's was not common in Europeans of his time, but it became a valuable asset for him when he explored new lands and met people of new and unfamiliar cultures.

The customs and laws of the people he encountered interested Amerigo. Nevertheless, he didn't hesitate to denounce the horror of some of their ways, which were as barbarous as the land was pleasant and fertile.

"I saw a city where pieces of salted human flesh were hung from the beams of houses just as we hang sausages and smoked boar meat in our kitchens," wrote Vespucci. After going ashore, the crews were sometimes met by groups of clubwielding women sent in reconnaissance.

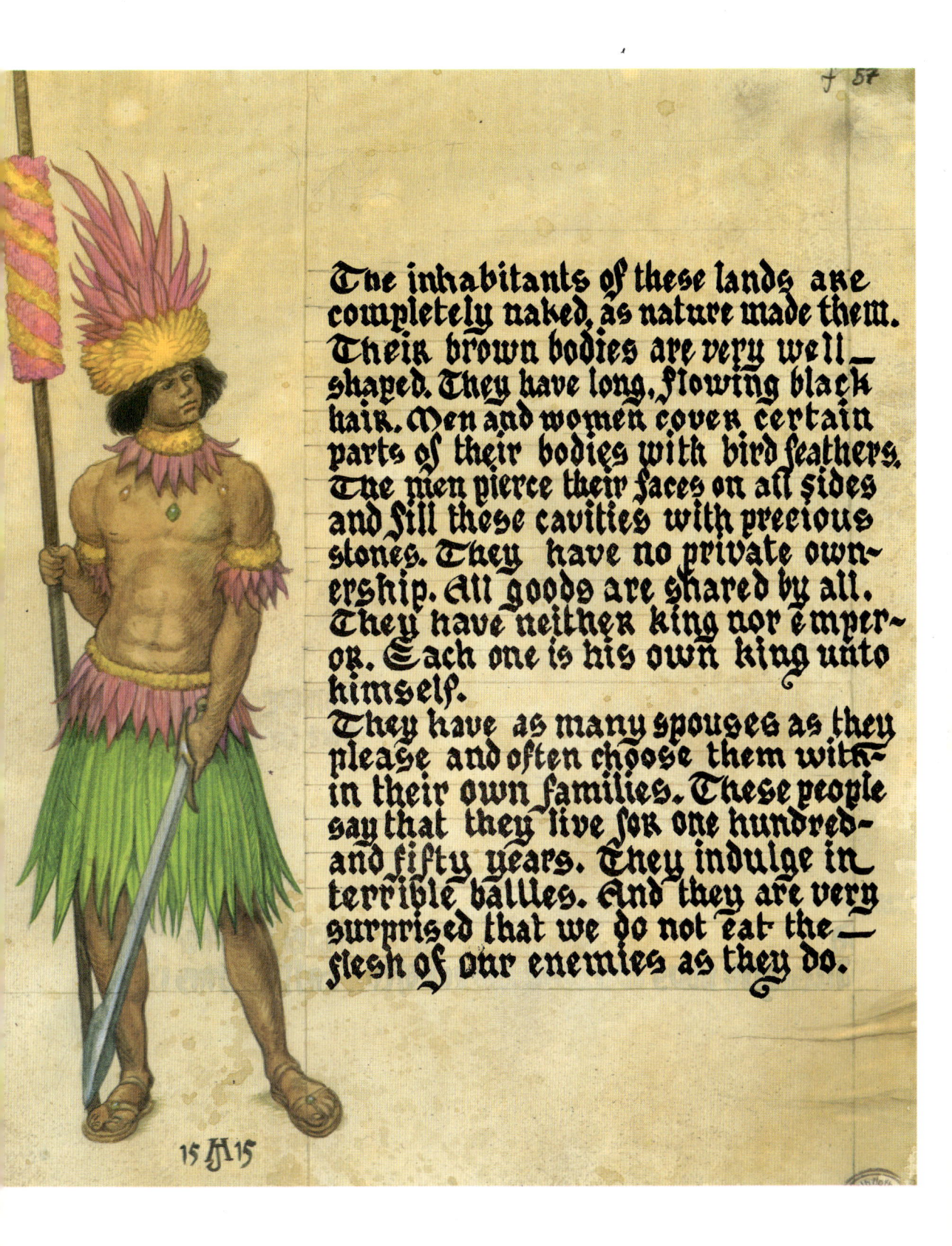

The inhabitants of these lands are completely naked, as nature made them. Their brown bodies are very well-shaped. They have long, flowing black hair. Men and women cover certain parts of their bodies with bird feathers. The men pierce their faces on all sides and fill these cavities with precious stones. They have no private ownership. All goods are shared by all. They have neither king nor emperor. Each one is his own king unto himself.

They have as many spouses as they please and often choose them within their own families. These people say that they live for one hundred and fifty years. They indulge in terrible ballies. And they are very surprised that we do not eat the flesh of our enemies as they do.

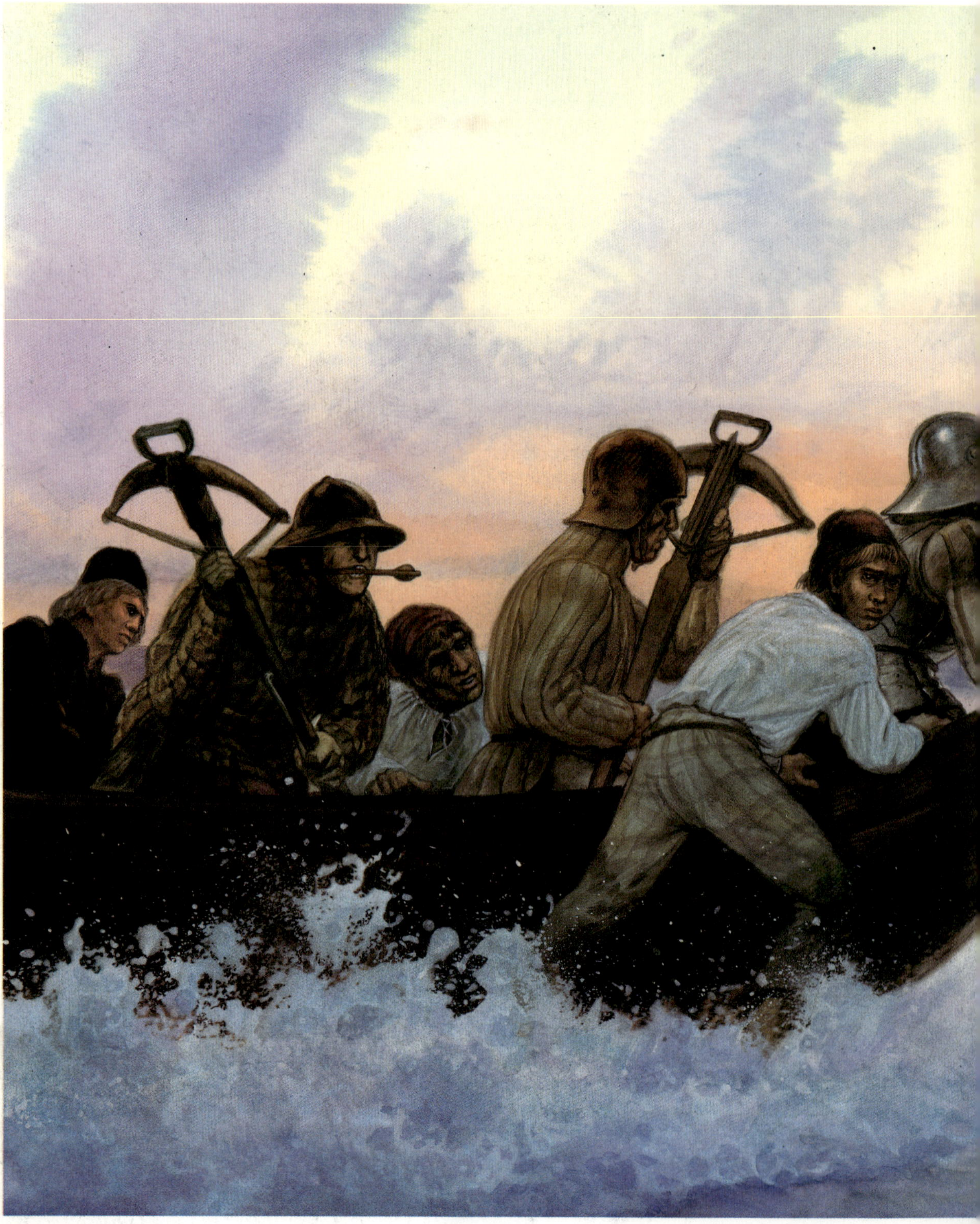

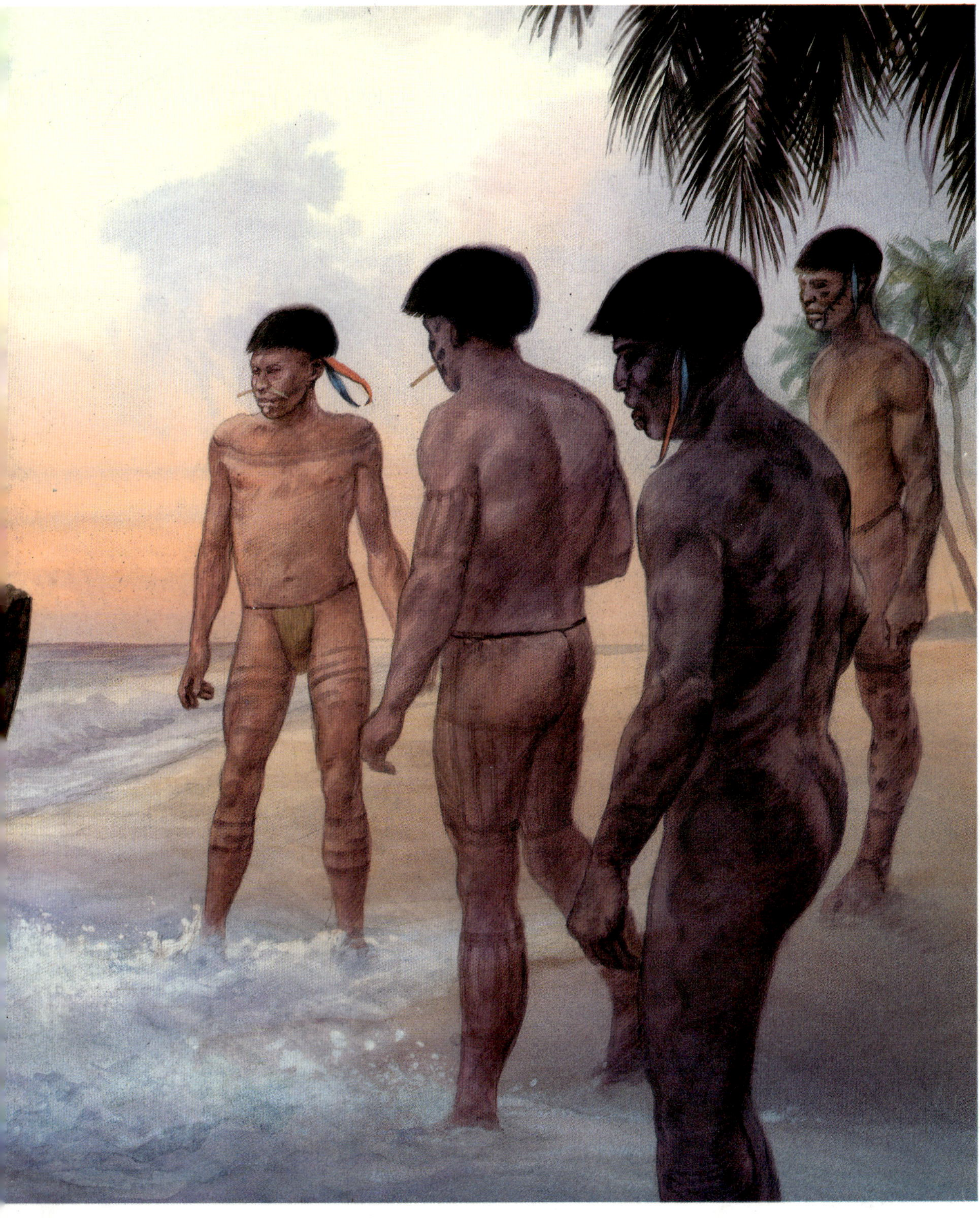

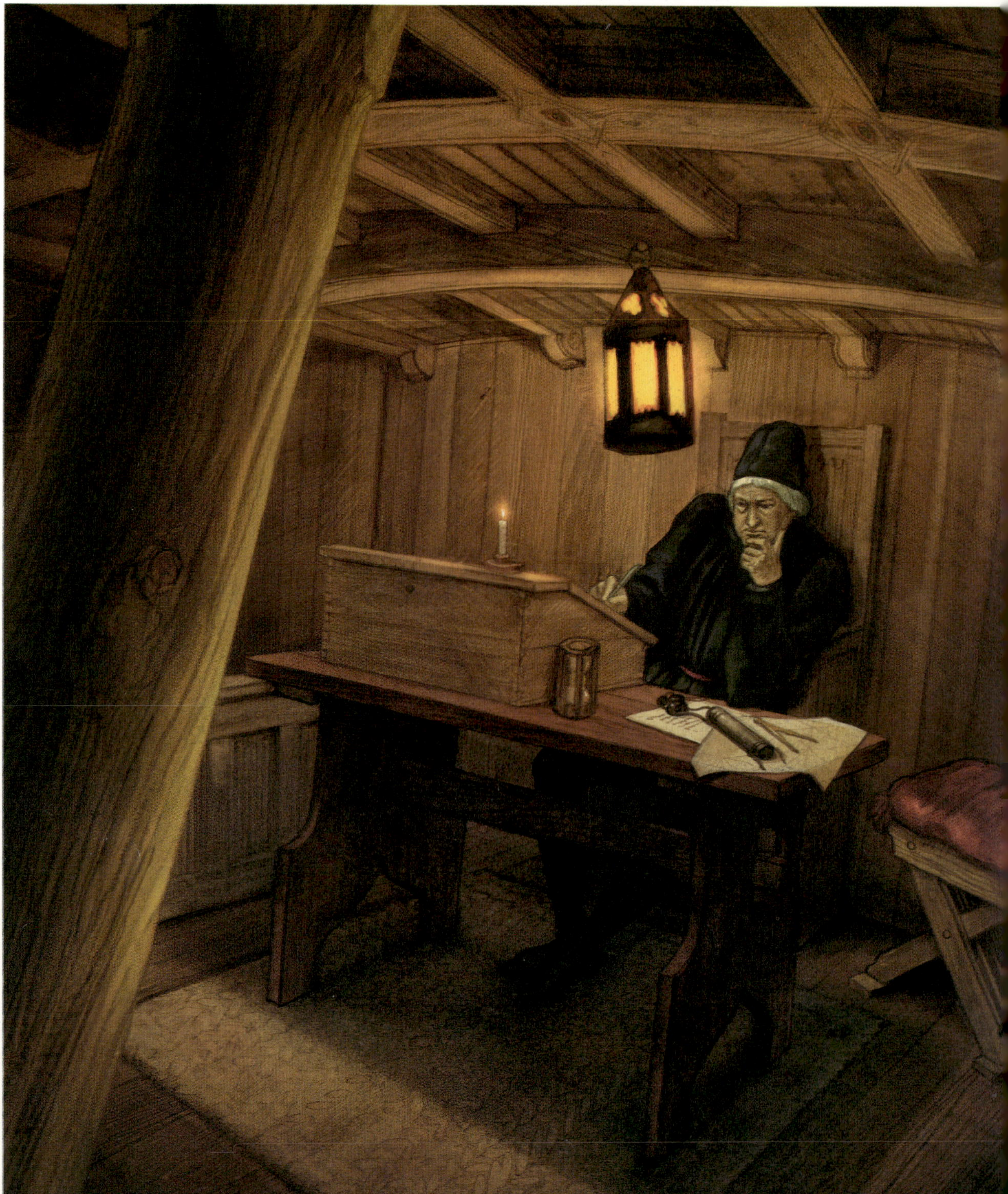

VESPUCCI

"One evening, some men went ashore to find water, but they came back immediately without having been able to reach the forest that bordered the beach. Several moments later, their boat touched the hull of the ship. As soon as I saw the second mate on the gangway, I knew that something terrible had just happened; one man was missing at roll call that night. For the first time, I had to enter in the logbook that the Indians had been hostile and killed one of us. However, as it was our mission, we continued our exploration, but we were not able to have a funeral for our unfortunate companion."

Amerigo was making enormous progress toward reaching the goal that he was pursuing in King Manuel's service. All conquests made within the 370 leagues to the west of the Cape Vert Islands legally belonged to Portugal, according to the Treaty of Tordesillias of 1494. While offering new possessions to Portugal, Amerigo was also going to show that the earth was round, and that it was possible to circumnavigate it. Although other learned men had said this before, no one had been able to prove it.

اسطرلاب   astrolabe

Upon Amerigo's return from the new land, others, far from the sea in Europe, were also discussing exploration. Poets, philosophers, and cosmographers were assembled at the Duke of Lorraine's court. They didn't know the sea; nevertheless, they debated the results of the voyages of discovery, which interested the princes, financiers, and merchants. Some of them, taking the side of Spain, rejected the idea of a new continent, but others sided with Portugal, maintaining that Christopher Columbus had not discovered a continent but only a simple archipelago on the Indies route.

In the Vosges region in 1505, the library of Saint-Die was the scene of great excitement. Many learned men came to discuss the world's geography. Gauthier Lud, Duke Rene II's secretary, attentively studied his globe, and began to question the world as the people of that time knew it. Although Lud was convinced that Columbus's information challenged Ptolemy's geographic affirmations, a belief that he shared with numerous cosmographers, he couldn't explain why. His questions remained unanswered until he was brought a manuscript signed by Amerigo Vespucci. After reading it, Gauthier Lud gathered his friends together in the chapter library. There, he told them of this stranger, Vespucci, and of the amazing, valuable discoveries Vespucci had made about the world.

africa
Cabo Verde
mare oceanum
India
auster
circulus antarcticus

During my third voyage, I studied the sky and its planets, which I carefully noted. Today, it is evident that we have measured the fourth part of the heaven's canopy and have discovered land. This land is a continent formerly unknown to Europeans and which, contrary to widespread belief, separates Europe from the Indies.

Amerigo's manuscript, written for the Medicis on his return to Portugal, swept away the doubts of the scholars of Saint-Die. With his scientific observations, the Florentine navigator had cleared up the mystery of the hidden face of the heavens, which could only be observed by going around the world. In sailing from north to south Amerigo had observed new stars, which led him to hypothesize the existence of two hemispheres. However, it was difficult to judge the truth of these assertions at such a great distance from the reality described by the navigators. For assistance in this task, Gauthier Lud and his friends asked the philosopher Mathias Ringmann and the cartographer Martin Waldseemuller, both greatly experienced in these matters, to join them.

In 1507, after more than two years of discussion, the learned men of Saint-Die published a new cosmography largely inspired by Amerigo's writings, replacing Ptolemy's vision of the world.

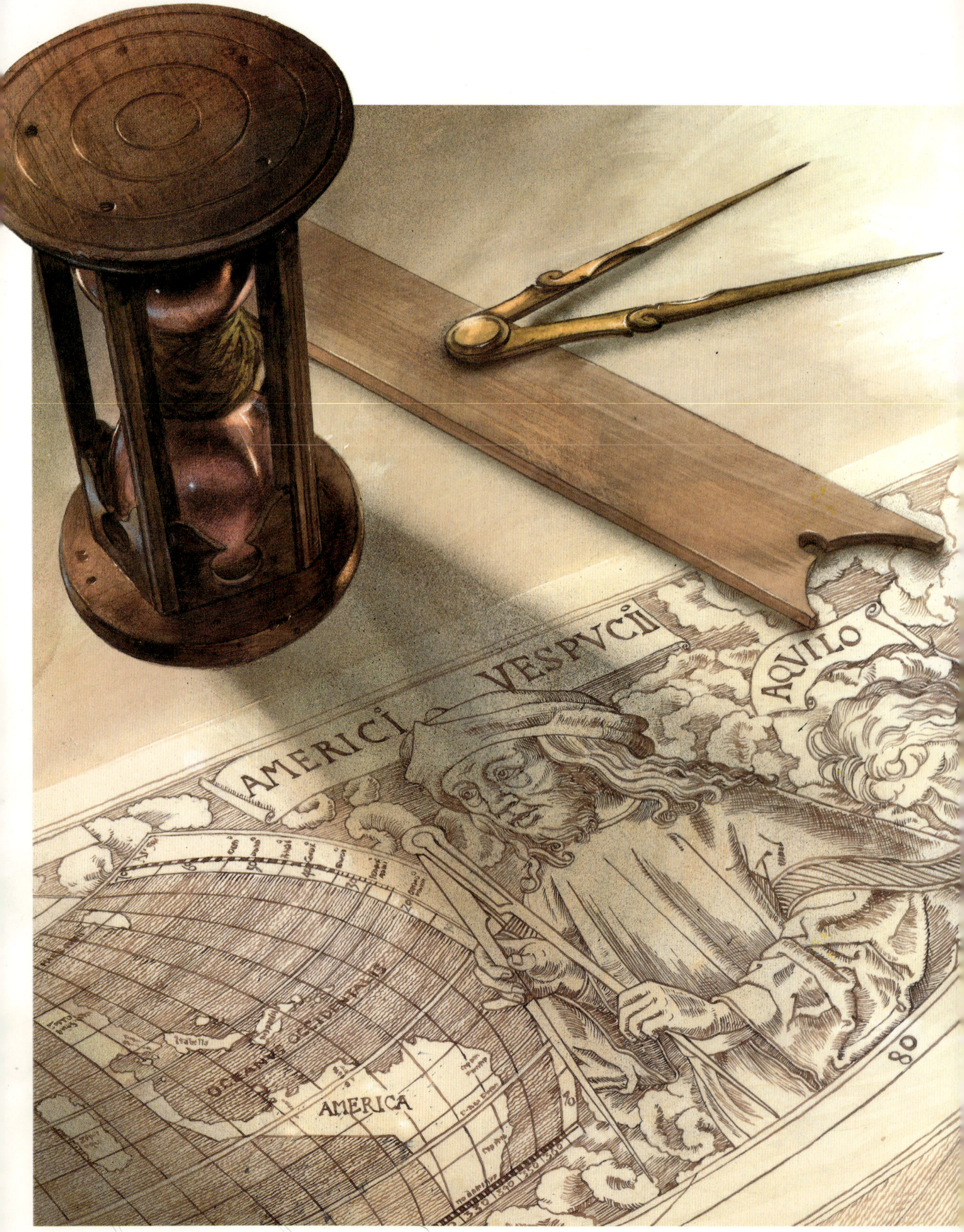
AMERICI
VESPVCII
AQVILO
AMERICA
80

Although Amerigo hadn't sailed around the extremity of the new continent, Martin Waldseemuller drew its outline after having read the descriptions of the voyages. In 1507, Waldseemuller was the first to apply the name "America," in honor of Amerigo, to the New World.

It wasn't until 1522, however, that Magellan's expedition circled the globe, the first in history to do so. By passing Cape Horn, Magellan also opened up the most famous maritime route. This new exploit confirmed Amerigo's conclusions once and for all. Soon, the charts incorporating "America" had been distributed throughout Europe. The *Cosmography of Saint-Die* explained:

"Today, Europe, Africa and Asia have been more thoroughly explored. But there is a fourth part of the world which was discovered by Amerigo Vespucci. As each of the other lands was named after a woman, we see no reason why this other land should not be called Amerige, in other words: the land of Amerigo or America, for the wise man who discovered it."

Sixteen years had gone by since Amerigo had first gazed at the wind-filled sails of Columbus's caravels. Having become the director of the Records of Spanish Conquests, the Florentine navigator could be proud of his success, but fame didn't affect his rigor and humility. This gentleman, whom Christopher Columbus had called the "modern messenger of voyages of exploration," died on February 22, 1512, at the age of sixty-one.

Today, historians are divided in their view of Amerigo Vespucci's exploits. Some question the number of his voyages; others doubt that they even took place. However, going beyond the questions raised about the discovery of America, few could deny that Amerigo Vespucci was an enlightened and scientific man. His humanistic values refused to let the temptation of material riches divert himself from his destiny. He was a man ahead of his time.

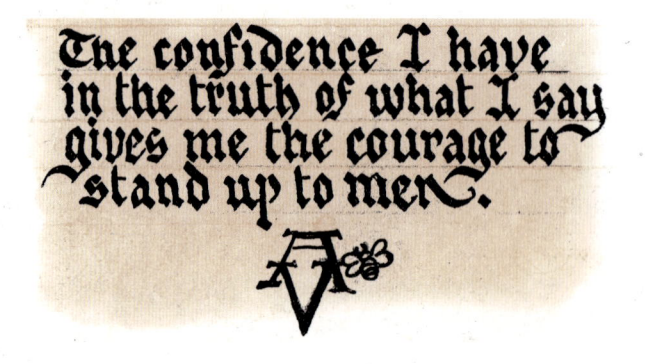

> The confidence I have in the truth of what I say gives me the courage to stand up to men.

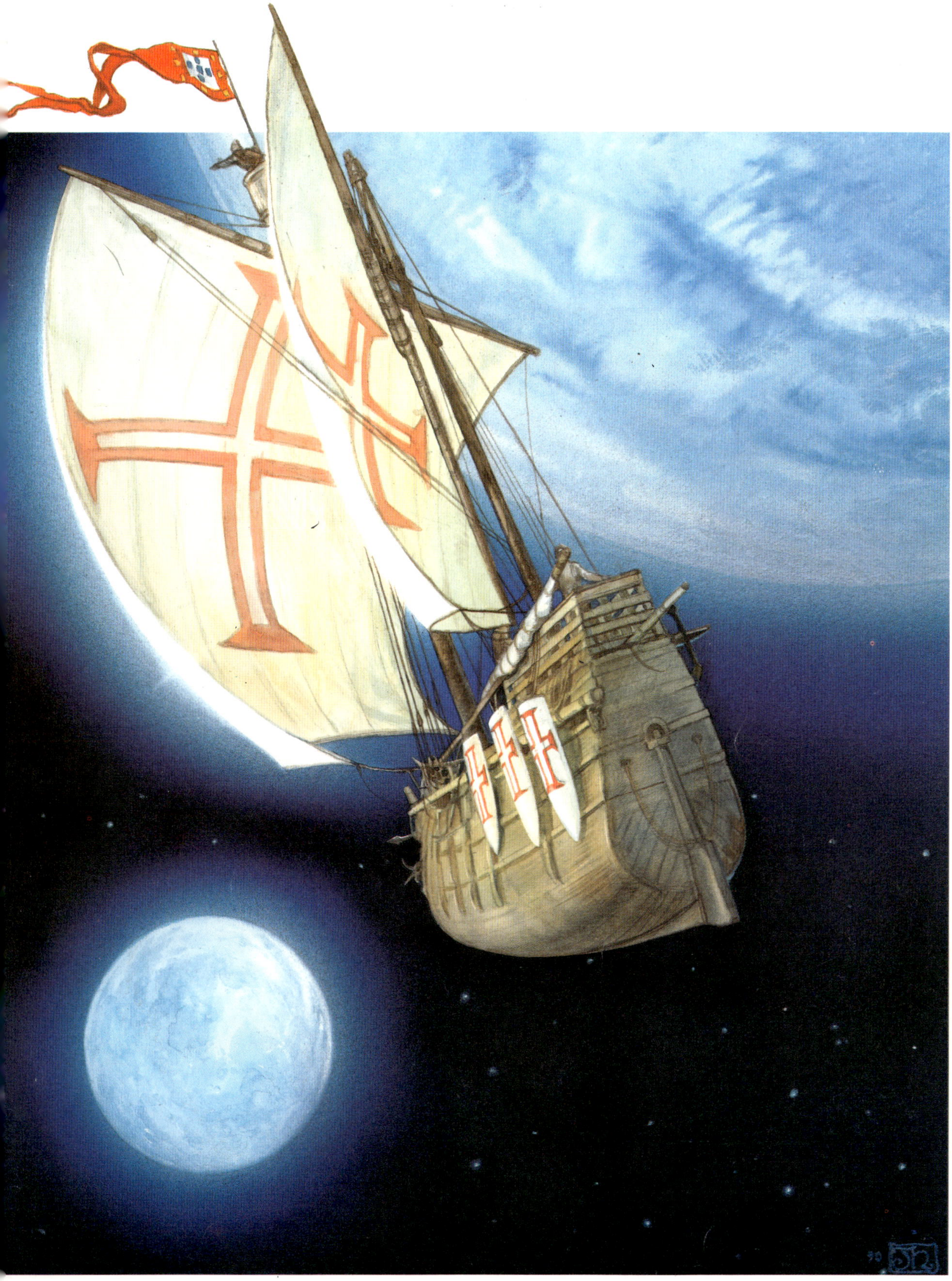

TERRA INCOGNITA

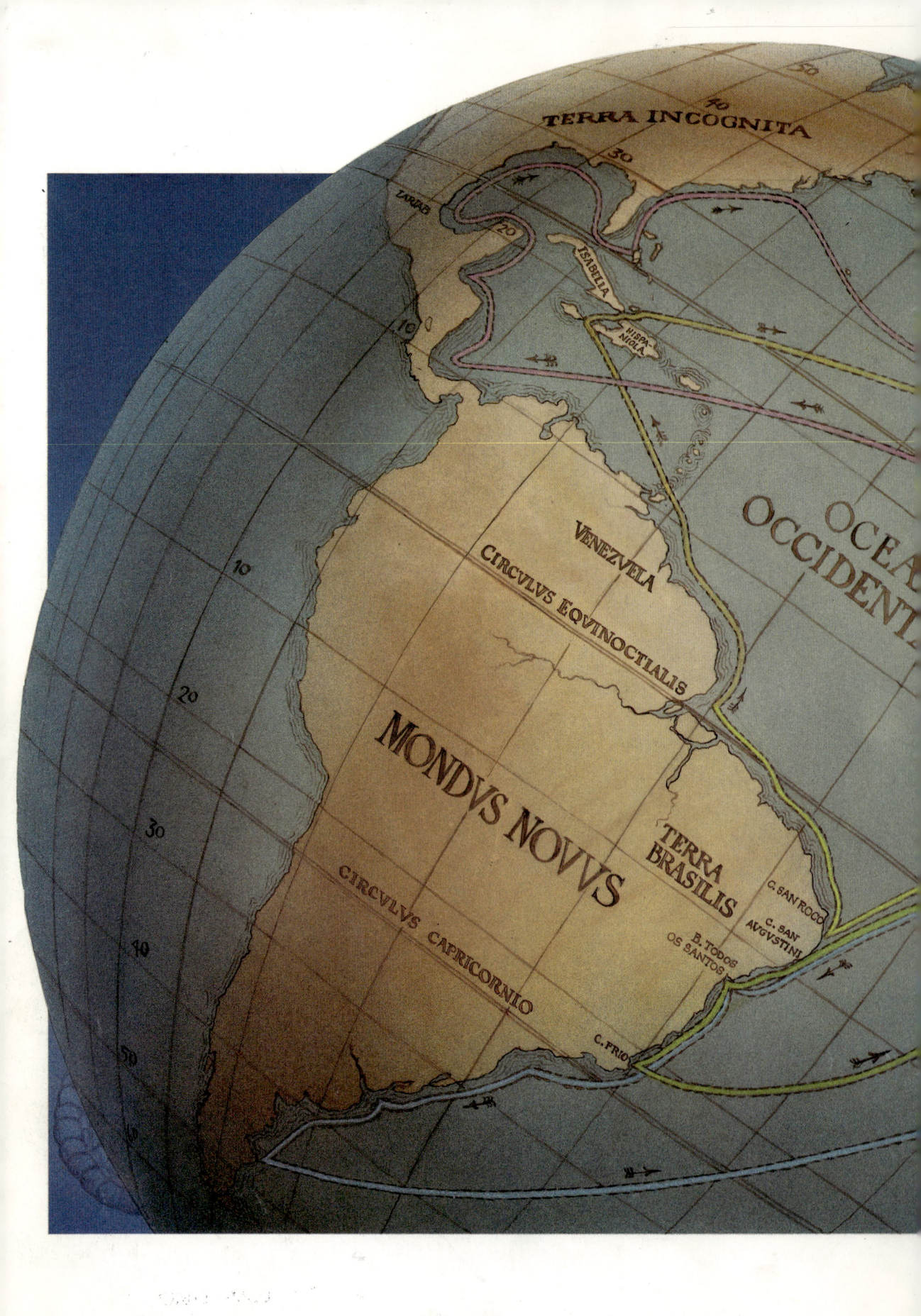

ZARAB

ISABELLA

HISPA-
NIOLA

OCEA
OCCIDENTA

VENEZVELA
CIRCVLVS EQVINOCTIALIS

MONDVS NOVVS

TERRA
BRASILIS

C. SAN ROCO
C. SAN
AVGVSTINI
B. TODOS
OS SANTOS

CIRCVLVS CAPRICORNIO

C. FRIO

THE VOYAGES OF VESPUCCI

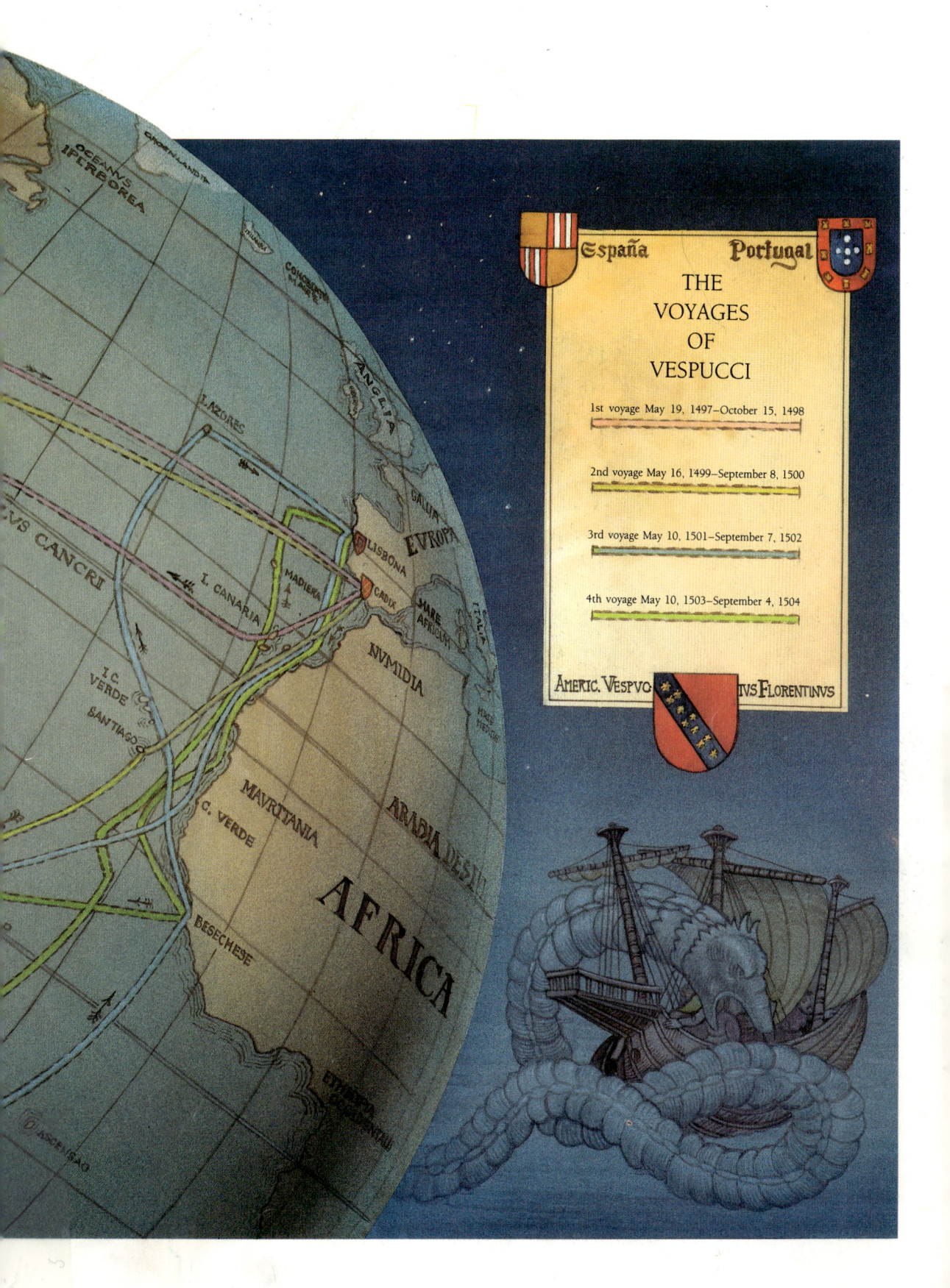

1st voyage May 19, 1497–October 15, 1498

2nd voyage May 16, 1499–September 8, 1500

3rd voyage May 10, 1501–September 7, 1502

4th voyage May 10, 1503–September 4, 1504

AMERIC. VESPVCIVS FLORENTINVS

VESPUCCI

PERSPECTIVE

1450–Gutenberg invents printing
1451–Columbus's birth in Genoa
1452–Vespucci's birth in Florence
1453–Fall of Constantinople
1486–Dias crosses the Cape of Tempests, today called the Cape of Good Hope
1497–Vespucci's first voyage, for Spain
1498–Vasco da Gama reaches India via the East
1499–Vespucci's second voyage, for Spain
1501–Vespucci's third voyage, for Portugal
1503–Vespucci's fourth voyage, for Portugal
1506–Columbus's death in Spain
1507–Vespucci's fifth voyage (not substantiated)
1512–Vespucci's death in Seville
1519–Magellan's departure for the first voyage around the world

The handwritten texts on pages 7, 17, 24, 28, are from Amerigo Vespucci's letters.

JB   Jaeger, Gerard.
Vespucci   Vespucci
            W

GOSHEN PUBLIC LIBRARY
601 SOUTH FIFTH STREET
GOSHEN, IN 46526-3994